Godliness is Great Gain

Author unknown

Originally published in the 1800's
by the American Tract Society

D1490612

Grace & Truth Books

Sand Springs, Oklahoma

ISBN # 1-58339-051-0
Originally published in the 19th century by the American
Tract Society
Printed by Triangle Press, 1996
Current printing, Grace & Truth Books, 2004

Cover art by Caffy Whitney
Cover design by Ben Gundersen
Interior drawings by Greg Gundersen

Grace & Truth Books
3406 Summit Boulevard
Sand Springs, Oklahoma   74063
Phone: 918 245 1500

www.graceandtruthbooks.com

Table of Contents

"Move that pile of boxes to the other room, boy."

Chapter 1

THE WORK-HOUSE APPRENTICE

When Robert was ten years old, a shopkeeper in Cornwall, England was looking for an apprentice. During this time an apprentice did the work of a slave. This was the only type of life that Robert could expect since he was an orphan. The shopkeeper needed a boy to carry out the hardest chores given to the youngest and lowest person in the shop. Robert would do just that.

During ancient times, the life of an orphan was much different from today. Orphanages did not exist, so Robert was left to his own risk at a very young age. Like all other orphans, Robert went from one work house to another. This was his only way to survive. The owners of work houses did not feel it was their job to give the unwanted children any schooling or spiritual instruction. Thus Robert knew very little about reading and writing, and he knew even less about godly things.

From morning till night his back-breaking duties never ceased. One superior would say, "Move that pile of boxes to the other room, boy."

Then another one would walk by and say, "Don't you know anything? Leave those boxes right where they are!"

When Robert followed the latest set of orders, the first man would kick him and say, "You are the laziest dog alive."

Robert tried to be patient with them, even though they didn't think he deserved so much as a polite word.

Robert was not one to complain. He accepted his lot in life and was thankful that it wasn't worse. He had heard sad stories of other boys who were trying to survive their bondage. Mr. Vincent gave Robert enough food but little time to eat it. When his hard day ended, he was allowed to sleep under the counter. He had blankets to keep warm and clothes that were decent. In many ways this was the finest setting Robert had ever known.

There was one thing that Robert lacked, though. Perhaps he didn't realize it because it had been missing all of his life. As far as he could remember, he had never had a friend. The isolation that he felt in this new home seemed normal. He managed not to let it bother him. There were a few times, however, when Robert's thinking was less than innocent. If someone was needlessly cruel, a plan of revenge sometimes flitted through the young boy's imagination. Most often, however, he was patient while being mistreated.

Whatever his natural talents and tastes were, his surroundings did little to develop them. Most people saw Robert as nothing more than a chore-boy. He didn't picture himself in a much better light. It is surprising, however, that he developed some very good habits on his own. He was hard-working, obedient, and truthful. Most likely, someone trained him very carefully in his earlier years. Robert couldn't remember who that was, and no one else cared.

All the young men who worked for Mr. Vincent had Sundays to themselves. If they chose, they could eat meals with the Vincent family. They did whatever suited them in their free time. Often they had little parties among themselves, but invited only their close friends. No one asked the work-house boy to join them, and this only separated him more. Robert's independence grew stronger. He had no real ties to anyone he knew and had no desire to seek friends elsewhere.

After helping the cook, Robert usually spent his Sundays by taking a long walk alone. Sometimes he occupied his time by creating little toys and this brought him his only joy. His only tool was a common pocket-knife. His materials were bits of wood and rubber and some spools that he gathered while sweeping the shop. He saved some of his first inventions. They revealed his delightful imagination, which had never been given a chance to develop. At that time Robert had no idea that the Sabbath had any higher purpose.

There was one time which he will probably always remember. While enjoying one Sunday outing, the sound of singing in the distance drew his attention. His first thought was to turn and run. He wanted to avoid the crowd of people whose voices joined in a sacred hymn. However, there was something pleasing about it. His curiosity won out and he moved toward the sound. Soon he found himself standing outside the largest assembly of people he had ever seen.

When the singing stopped, one man walked to the front and opened a large book. From that book the man read the most wonderful words that poor little Robert had ever heard. When the reader finished, he closed the book and spoke in a very serious and pleading tone. Praying was as new to Robert as the scriptures were. He had found something that interested him and he decided not to leave until he heard everything. After they sang another hymn, the man preached a moving sermon. Before the group left, the man announced there would be services again in several other places. Some services would be in the morning and some at night the next week.

Robert broke away before the crowd of people moved too far in his direction. He went home by a secluded path. Anxious thoughts and new desires to which he was a stranger awoke in his mind. He still was in the dark about the Being whose mercy he should seek. He only had vague ideas of Who is "the way, the truth, and the life." That night Robert experienced the beginning of that good work of the Holy Spirit in his heart. God would never give it up, but carry it on to perfection. Philippians 1:6 says, "Being confident of this very thing, that he which hath begun a good work in you will perform it until the day of Jesus Christ."

Naturally, Robert earnestly desired more direction. He knew no other way of finding it than going to the other places where services were being held. He knew that he couldn't go to the evening meeting. He didn't finish his work until everyone else in the house was in bed. Since he usually rose early to take a bath, he hoped they might let him go to the morning service. For the first time in his years as an apprentice, he became courageous enough to ask a favor.

The man Robert asked was the foreman, Mr. Thomson. He was a reliable man with good morals, but he was also very stern and rigid. Also, he looked down somewhat upon servants like Robert.

"You want to go out! Where do you want to go?" quizzed the foreman.

"I want to go to a morning church service on Maple Street."

The foreman didn't ask why, but gave his permission on one condition. Robert had to return in time to sweep the shop before it opened.

Now, for a good purpose, Robert awoke at the first light of dawn. He did as much work as possible before he left. Then he hurried away to drink in the instruction for which he now hungered and thirsted. After tasting the wonder of worshipping God, he took every opportunity to enjoy it again.

The change worked in the poor little boy proved to be true. It was obvious to anyone who cared to notice. The psalmist wrote, "The entrance of thy words giveth light; it giveth understanding unto the simple," Psalm 119:130. Once he tasted that the Lord is gracious, as a new creature, he continually desired to fulfill his new nature. Robert didn't let any chance slip by. He grew in grace and in the knowledge of our Lord and Saviour Jesus Christ.

Godliness is Great Gain

True religion is active and effective. It is like a bit of yeast in a lump of dough. It leavens the whole lump the same way true religion brings about a complete change in a person's heart. It not only changes what is evil, it also overcomes our indifference. Knowing God in a personal way causes everyday activities to become Christian delight. Truthfulness and obedience spring from the heart as unto the Lord. This is what Robert was experiencing.

Religiously, he had very few advantages. He had no Bible, and was a stranger altogether to Christian terms and discussion. In fact, the only religious instruction that he received was what he heard in public. Thankfully, what he did hear was true to God's word. He heard at the meeting that salvation is found in Christ alone through faith in Him. He heard that our duties must be performed faithfully. He treasured these things in his heart. By the teaching of the Holy Spirit, his trust was confirmed in the Saviour of sinners. He learned how he "ought to walk and to please God."

When the Holy Spirit fixes a person's eye of faith on Christ, their attitude changes. Often they find that they want to learn more about everything and remember what they learn. Energy and hope spring up in everyday happenings. When Robert was young, someone taught him how to read just a little. During the first five years of his apprenticeship, he had barely even seen a book. When he did see one, he made no effort to read it. When he became excited about "the one thing needful," he began to realize the value of knowledge. He wanted to further his religious knowledge more than anything. Robert imagined how wonderful reading a Bible would be. He even thought it might be possible to get one of his own. Right away he started learning to read and spell.

No doubt Robert did his work faster and easier when he was grown old than when he was a ten-year-old boy. He changed because of his principles and his new way of life. He began to be more organized and work faster, which gave him more time to work on his schooling. He got up much earlier during the long summer days, so he could finish his work. Often he made it impossible for the others to keep him busy till late in the evening. With the extra scraps of time that he gained by doing this, he built on his store of knowledge. Even if no one noticed all of his improvements, he had the satisfaction of thinking about all the new things flowing through his mind.

His moodiness changed into patience, love and generosity by true religion. Even though he could plainly remember the unfair and often cruel treatment he had received, Robert harbored no resentful feelings. He took it with meekness and quietness. He found pleasure in helping his unkind superiors. The patience, gentleness, and kindness that showed he was changed started to have an effect on them. They became more civil toward him and began to look upon him with some respect.

Nevertheless, they didn't let the past die. Robert was after all a poor work-house apprentice, who slept under the counter in the shop. Needless to say, there were advantages to being singled out. Because most of his fellow-workers avoided him, they took no notice of where he went or what he did. This saved him from being ridiculed and also from the temptation of worldly entertainment. These could have been a snare in his way.

The outdoor services Robert had been so faithful in attending ended in autumn due to shorter days and uncertain weather. As the last of the various congregations scattered, Robert left his sacred spot depressed.

An elderly man and his wife had also attended the outdoor services regularly. They noticed that Robert always paid strict attention. They took this opportunity to speak to him. "Hello, young man. I am Mr. Worthing, and this is my wife, Claire. We noticed that you have been to almost all of the services, and we wanted to meet you. Would you like to come to dinner with us?"

Robert was not used to kind words and a friendly handshake. All his life, people had spoken to him in commanding tones. His heart grew warm with thankfulness. Robert looked back on that day years later. It was at that moment he understood the term "communion of saints." He thought that the love of the Saviour must have caused these kind people to notice him. He loved them because they loved Jesus. This was the beginning of a valuable friendship. The good old people took him home with them and helped and encouraged him in many ways.

Very soon after this meeting, Robert traded some of his simple but clever toys for a New Testament. Mr. Worthing told his wife, "It will make Robert feel good about his independence. He obtained the Good Book by the fruits of his own labor. The poor lad must have something to show for his own creations."

Robert did not stay alone in the shop at night. A small terrier dog slept there too. Robert's last job each night was to let the dog in before he went to bed. Then he put it back out early in the morning. When Robert was going about his usual routine one night, a young man named John stopped him. John had been working for Mr. Vincent only a short time. "Robert, I'm going to take this dog into my room tonight. The rats in there are terrible."

"If you don't mind, Sir," said Robert firmly but with respect, "Do you have permission from Mr. Vincent or Mr. Thomson?"

"How dare you ask me a question like that?" John demanded. "It's none of your business whose permission I have!"

"John, I can't let the dog leave without orders. If you want, I can go ask Mr. Thomson. He just went upstairs."

"You can just forget it. Take that for your arrogance," replied the young man, slapping Robert across the face. "I'll get you back sometime, you beggarly work-house apprentice."

Robert didn't resent the slap or the insult. He quietly shut the door and went to bed. In the middle of the night, the dog's low growl woke Robert. After listening for a while, he could clearly hear someone outside trying to open one of the side windows. He jumped up and got dressed. Before he could call for help, the dog barked and scared away the burglar. Robert stayed up to watch the rest of the night, but didn't hear the noises again.

Before the shop opened in the morning, Robert called Mr. Thomson and told him what happened in the night. After looking around, Mr. Thomson found clear proof that someone had indeed attempted a robbery. There was no doubt that the barking of the dog prevented it. Later, Robert saw the young man who had slapped him. He ventured, "It's a good thing, Sir, that you didn't take the dog last night."

"Yes," replied John. "It's a good thing. I'm really glad. It would have been odd for him not to be here that night of all nights in the year."

They fixed the window fasteners and gave the watchman orders to pay closer attention. The incident was soon forgotten. No one ever knew of Robert's encounter with John. If Robert had given John the dog, the robbers might have broken in. Then Robert would have been suspect as a partner in the crime. Mr. Thomson would have dealt with Robert harshly.

A few weeks later, Mr. Thomson went out for the evening. As usual, the shop was locked securely. It wouldn't be opened again except for the little side door through which Robert entered. Mr. Vincent didn't allow him to open it until bedtime. It was at this point that John demanded of Robert, "I need the key to the front door of the shop. I left my hat in there."

"I'm sorry, John," replied Robert. "You know that I can't give you the key."

"I don't know that. Just because of what happened the other night, you think you are better than everybody else. I demand you give me the key."

"I can't, John. Mr. Thomson trusted me with it, and I must be faithful to that trust."

Once again Robert stood up to the threats and insults of the bully. Finally John said, "Oh never mind! I can get my hat in the morning."

Mr. Thomson came back earlier than Robert expected. Robert good-naturedly asked, "Can I go fetch a hat that John left in the shop?" He and Mr. Thomson went to the shop, but they couldn't find the hat. Instead they found a package of valuable items left ready to be taken out. Of course this alarmed Mr. Thomson, so he searched John's room. They found a large amount of stolen property. John was dismissed from his job immediately.

The easiest way to put an end to the stupidity of foolish men is to keep doing what is right. This often replaces prejudice with lasting respect. Robert's good conduct gradually wore away the sarcasm directed toward him because of his humble beginnings. This was especially true in Mr. Thomson's case, because he was an upright and considerate man. He was more and more convinced of Robert's trustworthiness.

A man's good conduct over a period of time gives him an advantage. Robert's firmness and loyalty had defended Mr. Vincent's property against thieves. Mr. Thomson decided it would only be fair to tell his employer about it.

"Mr. Vincent, I would like to make a suggestion about young Robert."

"Do you mean the work-house apprentice?" asked Mr. Vincent.

"Yes, he has been very loyal to us, and I believe he deserves a promotion."

Robert was relieved of the lowly kitchen work and was assigned work in the shop. Until then, Robert's pay was his clothing and food. Now Mr. Vincent gave him a new outfit suited for his new job and an annual salary.

Robert was most thankful for one part of the new arrangement. It was the one which showed the confidence Mr. Vincent had in him. Mr. Vincent still wanted Robert to sleep in the shop. However, he ordered a small room adjacent to the shop made into a comfortable bedroom for Robert.

There were still some young men in the shop too proud to consider themselves equal with a work-house apprentice. Robert had opportunities to show forgiving kindness for someone who had been haughty toward him. Then the proud feelings of the young men ended.

A worker named James Darwin was taken ill with a dangerous fever. He could not be safely moved from the house. All of his friends avoided his room in fear of catching his illness. Mr. Vincent hired a nurse to take care of him, but she soon quit. When no one could be persuaded to take such a dangerous position, Robert modestly offered, "I will take care of James."

"You are taking a dangerous risk. His illness is severe."

"I will run that risk for the sake of my fellow shopman!" he dutifully replied.

Robert's kind offer was accepted. He was put in charge of the sick youth. Under the instructions of the doctor, Robert proved to be a devoted and efficient attendant. Amazingly, the fever did not affect his own health. Robert had the satisfaction of seeing James gain back his health after a long and difficult struggle.

A warm and lasting friendship grew between the patient and his nurse. Others began to see Robert in a far better light. During Robert's remaining years at the shop, he was treated with the respect his actions earned. 1 Timothy 6:6 says, "But godliness with contentment is great gain."

The dangerous illness and the kindness that he showed James were the key to opening Robert's future advancement. Mr. Vincent sent for the young man's father, who stayed in town till his son had recovered. Since there wasn't room in the shop-quarters for him, Mr. Darwin stayed with the Worthings. These were the good old people who had been so kind to Robert. The couple told Mr. Darwin about Robert's character and past. They showed him the clever creations that Robert had traded for his New Testament.

"These are rough, but they show a promising talent. With some encouragement, he could become a success."

Mr. Darwin had many connections and made an arrangement. When Robert finished his contract with Mr. Vincent, he would go to work for an engineer in Northern England. Mr. Darwin's faith in Robert's abilities was proved right by his success in his new position.

More than fifty years after entering Mr. Vincent's shop as a work-house apprentice, Robert retired to one of the northern provinces. He had a successful business career and a loving family. His family could afford any worldly possession they wanted, but they remained unselfish. Their belongings were sacred, because they observed what the Lord says in Proverbs 3:9. "Honour the Lord with thy substance, and with the firstfruits of all thine increase."

They were humble and grateful for their blessings. They knew that God was the giver of all, and for His glory they sought everyone's enjoyment. They set their table modestly and opened their purse in charity, not greediness or recklessness. To them, leisure was a time to do good, and they cherished responsibility. Their possessions were managed instead of owning them. They directed both their expenses and savings to the "great account." Several projects were started to help the needy, relieve the distressed, and teach the unlearned. Bibles and tracts were given out to carry the gospel into the darkest corners of the country and through all the earth.

The head of that prosperous and virtuous family was poor Robert, the former Cornwall work-house apprentice.

He took off his coat and folded it up on his desk.

Chapter 2

OUR FELLOW CLERK

We always thought Henry Westerton was considered to be very mean. He was the assistant manager in the business where my cousin and I worked. He drew a handsome salary and he wasn't married. This did not seem to make him any more generous with his wallet. Not one of us would have wanted to be guilty of the terrible habits of which Mr. Westerton was guilty. When I say "one of us," I mean the dozen or so clerks who worked in our office. They came from their various houses everyday at nine o'clock to the large, crowded building in the city.

There could be no doubt that Henry Westerton was stingy. The careful way in which he brushed his hat every time he took it off proved it. It was an old-fashioned hat, but it was still in very good shape. Actually, he had a strange way with his hat. Once he was even seen inking the edges.

He wore the same coat to the office for three continuous years. He treated the coat as if he had only bought it last week. He took it off and folded it up on his desk. Then he put on an old office coat. He said the old, loose coat was more comfortable for writing. We were sure he did this because he was stingy and miserable.

We would try to tease him about his old hat and coat and other things, but it was all in vain. He was not irritated easily. He was so good-natured that he could handle almost anything. He was willing to be generous in everything except money. Of course, this only made teasing him more enjoyable.

Godliness is Great Gain

It wasn't only that Westerton wore old clothes. Some of us who only made a quarter of his pay would be ashamed of dressing as he did. However, it was the way Westerton showed his selfishness.

We did not get many holidays, but one summer on the birthday of King George the Fourth, we took one. We made reservations for a boating trip. Everyone except Westerton agreed to take a day off to sail up to Richmond. The manager and two other clerks who did not want to go cheerfully helped pay their share of the reservation fee. Westerton mumbled that he wished he could afford to go. He said he could not join us or help pay for any expenses. The general agreement was that he was even more selfish than everyone thought. For a long time afterwards we hinted about his selfishness, but he paid no attention to our remarks.

Soon it was discovered that Mr. Westerton was engaged. He and the young lady had been planning to get married for several years. She was waiting until he could afford to marry her.

We all knew the amount of Westerton's salary. There were many people who got married and lived comfortably on less than half of his large income. It was quite plain that only his greediness kept him from taking a wife. Of course, it was his lady's lack of sense, whoever she was, that made her put up with his delays. Excuses could be made for her. There were none for him, except that he was stingy.

This is not to say that Westerton was not generous at times. We must do the justice of giving him that credit. Once, one of our clerks suffered a long illness. He had a wife and family to support. While he was unable to work his financial situation became very bad. The manager gave him a small weekly paycheck and all the clerks donated money to help him as much as possible. Westerton gave a donation as well, though no one expected this of him.

Later, to our surprise, it was learned that he had done much more than anyone knew. When Mr. Smith returned to work, he gave us an unbelievable report about Mr. Westerton. He told us about how Westerton had visited him often. Money out of Westerton's pocket paid to keep Mr. Smith's oldest boy in school. Westerton would always bring something to cheer him. He had also paid a month's rent for Mr. Smith. The owner could have turned the Smith family out of their home or taken their furniture as payment.

This changed our opinion of Mr. Westerton slightly. Then one clerk accused Westerton of begging and taking donations for Mr. Smith from his friends. Obviously, Mr. Westerton thought that being generous with other people's money would be a cheap way of getting a good reputation. So Westerton did not get much credit for generosity after all that he had done.

In spite of all this, I have to admit that we liked Henry Westerton. To Westerton's credit it must be said that besides being good-natured, he was conscientious, cheerful, and never used bad language. He advised us now and then when our conduct was not quite as it should be. We could not help respect him even though we thought he was stingy.

Mr. Westerton had a good influence on me especially. One of our clerks was a carefree, wild, young man. He almost persuaded me to go with him to Drury Lane Theatre one evening. I certainly would have gone, but Westerton heard of our plans. After work he kindly, yet seriously, spoke about the dangers and temptations to which I was about to expose myself. The grief it would cause my parents if I became involved in these amusements concerned him.

"Such pursuits often become the downward road to eternal ruin," he cautioned.

I had great cause to respect Mr. Westerton for his wisdom. That young man turned out very badly, and I could have also. It was so hard to figure how he could be so stingy. Mr. Westerton left the office building after many years. It seemed strange that, even though he had such a well-known reputation for being greedy, almost everyone was sorry when he left. At that time, none of us knew exactly where he went. We found out later that he became a partner in a large, flourishing business in the city.

This was the reason for his stingy and conserving ways, no doubt. Perhaps he had been saving and scrimping until he had money enough to purchase a share in that partnership. This was all right in itself, but we thought that a man could be careful and thrifty without being cheap.

Some time later, we read in the paper that Henry Westerton married the lady he had kept waiting all these years. We didn't envy the lady.

Many years later, I was promoted to assistant manager at the office building. An old friend, who lived a few miles out of London, invited me to spend an evening at his home. I would then take an early train back to London in the morning.

Upon boarding the train, I noticed only one other person in the car. The face of the middle-aged gentleman puzzled me. I felt sure that I knew him or had met him somewhere. The mystery was soon solved, however. As soon as he spoke, I recognized the voice as belonging to Mr. Henry Westerton. I immediately introduced myself to him. Of course, I had changed considerably. We were soon engaged in a pleasant conversation.

It was difficult to persuade myself that this was the same Henry Westerton of earlier days. My recollection of him was the old, well-preserved hat and coat which seemed so much a part of him. Here he was in neat and expensive clothing. His outward appearance was that of a prosperous man. Perhaps the position he held required him to appear well dressed. He might still be stingy for all that.

These remarks were kept to myself, of course, while our conversation went on. After a little while, I found my suspicions and former prejudices melting away. Let me explain how and why.

Born to Christian parents, I was trained in "the nurture and admonition of the Lord." This Scripture verse has an important meaning. I hope that many of my readers know by experience what it means. By God's mercy and in answer to the prayers of my parents, I was saved from the bad influences of worldly companions. I wasn't free from temptations, however. When I was younger, I didn't walk in the way of the cross. "But God, who is rich in mercy, for His great love wherewith He loved [me], Even when [I was] dead in sins, hath quickened [me] together with Christ, (by grace [I was] saved)," Ephesians 2:4-5.

When I accidentally met my former supervisor, it was only right to tell him how thankful I was. He helped me that day when I wanted to go to the theater. His kind and gentle influence held me back from what might have been the beginning of a downward road.

We began a conversation which made us regret the short distance we had to travel together. Mr. Westerton got off the train at a station before London, where I was headed. He pressed his business card into my hand and gave me an urgent invitation to visit his home in that neighborhood.

The Christian fellowship we had just enjoyed made my early impressions of Westerton seem untrue. I certainly could not see how the two images fit together. His conversation mostly centered on the Christian religion, which is the direct opposite of selfishness. Scripture tells us in express terms that "the love of money is the root of all evil." His conversation showed his own generosity. However, his habit of saving and carefulness nobody could deny. His fellow clerks criticized him, in spite of their liking for him.

Godliness is Great Gain

"Oh well," I thought to myself. "The world is full of inconsistencies, and they often creep into the Christian church. There is no explanation for these things. The smartest thing to do is take warning when we notice them."

With Mr. Westerton's card safely in my pocket, I rode on trying to decide whether to accept his invitation on some future day.

In another fifteen minutes the train reached its destination. I took a carriage to the home of my friend and found there were other visitors besides myself. During the evening, Mr. Westerton's name was mentioned. To my astonishment, he was referred to as one of the most open-handed, generous men in the whole city.

"Do you mean the Henry Westerton who's name and address are on this card?" I asked, getting out the card and handing it to the one speaking.

"Yes, he's the same man. Do you know him?" he asked.

"I know him a little," I answered rather coldly. I could not help thinking that the praises I heard were not quite deserved. "Westerton is rich now," I thought. "He may not have the temptation to be stingy as he once did, but...."

"How long have you known him?" asked my friend, breaking into the current of my thoughts.

"I knew him several years ago when he was in a different position. I knew him much better than I do now. I met him again today, and he has invited me to renew our acquaintance.

"Which you will do, of course."

"I am not certain," I replied. "I would like to know more about him first."

The other guests fulfilled my wish by heaping glowing praises on Mr. Westerton. He was pictured as the perfect example of generosity. They estimated his income as very high indeed, adding that he lived simply so he could

*The other guests fulfilled my wish by heaping
glowing praises on Mr. Westerton.*

save all that he could. The report was that every year he gave away far more than he spent in his whole business establishment.

Personally active in every good word and work, his sympathy, as well as his financial help, made many sorrowful hearts leap for joy in thankfulness. He was the friend of the fatherless and widows, taking time to visit them in their distress. Many young men got their start in business with Mr. Westerton's help. Stories were told of others rescued from the edge of disaster and from the consequences of youthful mistakes. I learned that his own family was very happy. His wife accompanied him in the noble efforts of her husband in doing the work of religion and kindness.

After a pleasant hour had passed, almost everyone had gone. I was alone with my friend.

"My, but you are in a silent mood," he said, trying several times to draw me into further conversation.

I answered, "I am thinking of Mr. Westerton. I'm trying to understand the change which has taken place in his character. When I knew him, he had such reputation for penny-pinching."

"Penny-pinching!" exclaimed my friend in surprise. "He is the last person I would suspect of that!"

"The clerks in our office always thought he was cheap and greedy. We had chances daily to observe his conduct. If he is as you describe him, we may have made a mistake. Yet, I really cannot understand it."

"I cannot understand it, either," said my friend. "Perhaps," he added after a slight pause, "I can partly explain it. How did you come to form such an opinion of Mr. Westerton?"

At first I hesitated to answer my friend's question, but he urged me to explain. "I would not ask you," he said, "if I did not have a good reason. I hope I can remove the bad impression from your mind."

I told him about the cheap, miserable habits for which Westerton was noted. I told my friend how he watched every penny even though we knew he had a large salary.

"Then you never heard," my friend continued, speaking quietly, "that he might have had some particular reasons for such careful spending? Perhaps you did not know him very well, after all."

"If there had been any good reason, we would have known. It would have been easy for him to explain, but he never did. The problem explained itself when he left the office to join his present partners. Of course he had to pay for that."

"Oh!" said my friend.

"Besides," I added, "there was the young lady he kept waiting so many years until he could afford to marry her. I am glad they are happy now. It wasn't right to keep her waiting year after year. If what we heard was true, they set their wedding day very soon after the engagement. Westerton drew back and put it off until he was ready."

"That was true," said my friend, still very quiet. "Well, is that all?"

"That's quite enough to give us a bad opinion of him," I replied. "I can tell from your manner that you don't agree."

"The story is well known by now," my friend responded, "so I can tell you about it. Perhaps when you have heard what I have to say, you will see that your judgment was hasty. However, let me tell you, that Westerton did not pay a penny of capital to the firm he joined, because he did not have a penny. Here is my story."

Mr. Westerton entered life with very good prospects. His father was a banker in a large town in one of the western counties, and he was very rich. He had a large family and Henry was his oldest son.

A sudden, unexpected turn for the worse occurred as sometimes happens in business. The banker was utterly ruined. There is no need to give the details about that. Its effect on his mind was drastic. The banker became a helpless invalid. Out of all his family, only Henry was old enough or able to support himself. It was at this time that he was about to be married.

Young Westerton had two choices. One was to marry, and virtually abandon his family. They would be hardly able to survive on the little assistance he might give them. The alternative was to break off his engagement, leave his original job, and work to support his father, sisters, and brothers.

Unconcerned about himself, he explained the situation to the young lady who was to be his wife.

"If we cannot be married now," she said, "it is all right. However, there is no need to give up our engagement. When you feel you are able to claim me for your wife, I will be waiting. Until then...."

With that, they parted. The Westerton family moved to London. Henry worked at the office where you first met him. For ten years he struggled through difficulties which would have stopped many stronger men than he. He knew what was right and God gave him heavenly strength and wisdom. He accepted his task and denied himself luxuries so he could provide necessities for his father. He paid for his sisters' and younger brothers' education. He found jobs for them, encouraged them by his example to be honest and industrious, and protected them when they needed it.

"All this time," I said, feeling ashamed and guilty, "we were calling him mean and cheap. We were laughing at how he took care of an old hat and coat."

"That is the way we all are," replied my friend. "Man looks at the outward appearance. We have yet to learn how many noble, God-guided, and self-denying hearts beat under a very poor exterior. Shall I finish my story?"

"You don't need to," I said. "I can guess the rest."

"Well, there is not much more to tell. One after another, his brothers and sisters became able to provide for themselves. Still it was mainly the oldest son who supported their father. This burden became increasingly difficult to bear. An unexpected and extraordinary opportunity opened for Westerton to join the firm in which he is now the leading partner. It was plain to see that the strong and wonderful hand of God was in it. His kind treatment was payment for the caring he had shown to others. Now, do you still believe that your former supervisor was mean and greedy?"

It is enough for me to say that I have learned a lesson which I hope never to forget. One should never make hasty judgments when looking at outward appearances.

One last bit of advice to the reader: The present world does not always justly repay with either rewards or punishments. There is another world where everything that cannot be explained in this world will be explained. All that is imperfect will be made perfect and just. In all God's dealings with men, there is nothing more commonly seen than this. God smiles upon men who honor their father and mother and place their earthly interests above their own.

"Poor thing! The rain will soak her and the baby in no time at all."

Chapter 3

THE TWO JOURNEYS

"Looks like it's going to be a rainy night," said the Emerald's coachman. He was speaking to the young man sitting next to him in the coach-box. "Would you be kind enough to hold the reins while I put on my coat? It's going to be a stormy night, too," he added, as the breeze plucked at his cap. "There's a flash of lightning, looks like we will be in the middle of it soon."

"Actually," said Arthur Sutherland, "I don't mind a little dampness. Since there are no other inside passengers, however, can't you let the poor woman ride in there out of the rain?"

The "poor woman" looked thankfully at the young man, who spoke the words with kindness. He seemed to be enjoying the pelting rain which brought welcome relief from the hot July day. The cool rain was settling dust on the wide road. It stirred up a refreshing smell from the meadows and hedges nearby.

Our story took place in days long ago. Railroads were only a new topic of conversation, and oftentimes travelers, reporters, and the general public made fun of them.

The driver didn't have time to answer Arthur's question, because the young man suddenly became excited. A sharp flash of lightning was followed by a loud thunderclap. "That's beautiful," the young man exclaimed. The highbred horses reared and plunged in their harnesses as fast as they could go. They proved very quickly that the coachman was right about expecting a storm. The thunder, which startled the horses and sparked the attention of Arthur

27

Sutherland, startled the poor woman passenger. He heard a shriek behind him.

Arthur saw she was pale and trembling, and had only a thin summer cloak. Her other shawl was tied over her bonnet and spread around her baby, which she held close to her chest. Arthur knew that these clothes would not shelter her from the rain. It was now a steady downpour.

"You will let her get inside, won't you?" he asked kindly. "Poor thing! The rain will soak her and the baby in no time at all."

"We will be changing horses soon," replied the coachman. "Then I will see what I can do. The owners are very particular. If they ever found out I did such a thing, I would be punished. On a night like this, however...."

The coach drew up to the inn door as the coachman was speaking. They exchanged the four panting horses for a fresh team from the stable. The coachman moved the young woman and her baby to the inside of the coach, where they were much more comfortable.

The storm increased in fury as the evening drew on. The lightning was fearfully brilliant and did not pause for an instant. The thunder was terrifyingly loud and the rain poured down in torrents. The three or four outside passengers wrapped themselves in comfortable, waterproof coats; then they pulled their hats over their eyes. They silently hoped it would soon be over. Now and then they expressed their common fear that the horses wouldn't be able to stand it much longer. It was likely that the horses might bolt. Fortunately, this did not occur and they reached their next stop without any mishap. The thunderstorm had died down a little, but the rain was pouring down heavily. As the coachman threw the reins to the horse keeper, a waiter from the inn ventured out to the muddy road. He announced that the next coach would be there in half an hour. Supper was on the table if the passengers would like to get down and come inside.

Arthur Sutherland was glad for the chance to move about. He was very hungry, so he accepted the invitation. As he was about to enter the inn, something caught his attention. There was a loud, angry fight at the door so Arthur stopped to listen.

"Is she an inside passenger? That's all I want to know!" the manager yelled fiercely.

"No, Sir, she is not," said the coachman. "She has a baby and she's going all the way to Birmingham. She didn't wear warm enough clothing for the night journey in the rain. There was no one inside when the storm came on, so I thought there would be no harm."

A loud swearing interrupted the coachman's apology and explanation. The manager announced that the Emerald would soon have another driver, that is if the coachman didn't start paying attention and doing his job right. The angry man also insisted that the woman now owed an extra fee. He would make the coachman pay it this time.

"Here's a gentleman who will tell you when and why I put the woman inside." He pointed to Arthur, who had come forward a few steps.

The young gentleman then briefly explained the situation to the angry manager. The poor woman was put inside when the storm started because he himself had requested it. He added, "If she had stayed on the top of the coach, she would have been drenched to the skin."

"That doesn't matter," retorted the angry man who was clearly one of the coach's owners. His overbearing, defiant speech, however, was not fit for his gentlemanly dress. His temper had been roused, probably because he had not been expecting the Emerald that night. When it came, it had only a few passengers. He continued, "That doesn't matter at all. If the woman goes inside, she must pay inside fare. That's final." Returning to the coach door he gruffly told the woman her other choice if she did not move.

29

The reader may fairly doubt if any person would act so unkindly in these circumstances. The writer was on the coach top that night and watched the scene being described. If anything, he has given a mild version of the "gentleman's" behavior.

The young mother softly replied that she was unable to pay the extra fee. She prepared to step out into the soaking rain. Arthur Sutherland, who was not legally considered a man yet, gently intervened.

He said, "Surely you are not going to turn the poor woman and her baby out into the rain, Sir! Being exposed to it the whole night may cause her death. She is not used to traveling, and she has nothing but a thin shawl in which to wrap herself and her babe."

"I can't help that," said the owner sharply. He seemed to think the young traveler's interruption was unwanted meddling and he resented it. "The young woman should have thought of that before she bought a ticket."

"When the coach started, I did not think it would be stormy," the woman said in a soft, gentle voice. "Even if I had known it, I had nothing warmer to put on. I think that I will be alright," she added with downcast eyes. "If it weren't for my poor baby...." She wrapped the precious baby as snugly as she could in her shawl. She was stepping from the coach, when the young man interrupted again.

"It is a great shame," he said angrily. "I wouldn't have expected...."

"I would like to know what business you have to interfere, Sir," said the owner hotly. "You had better pay the inside fare for her yourself if you care so much about it."

"Very well, I will then," returned the young man. "Please keep your seat, my good woman. I'll make it all right."

"I wouldn't think of it, Sir," she said. Before she could protest any further, the owner and her young helper disappeared. While she was hesitating about what to do next, the coachman came forward. He told her that she was to keep her inside place the rest of the way.

"Come, Mr. Sutherland," shouted a voice from the inn. "You are going to eat with us, aren't you? Here's some good food. You'd better hurry, though. Someone will soon say, 'Time's up, gentlemen.'"

"Thank you," replied Arthur, "but I am not going to eat supper this evening." The extra fee had dipped into a wallet that was already thin. The poor woman didn't know the price that her young supporter paid in his generosity.

The drenching rain lasted the rest of the journey. With hopes of something better to follow, Arthur tried to stop his hunger pains by munching a dry biscuit. If the woman knew, she would probably not have passed the night as comfortably as she did. Hours passed. The Emerald drove up to the office of the Hen and Chicks. Among others that early morning, a pleasant looking, manly young mechanic was waiting for the coach's arrival. A gleam of satisfaction passed over his face as he searched the roof of the coach.

"I am glad she didn't travel here through the terrible storm last night," he said to a fellow workman by his side. "She is delicate and timid. She doesn't have very warm clothes either. And the poor baby...."

"Here, Alex," the sound of his wife's voice came from the open coach window. It stopped the young man's speech, and he quickly ran to open the door.

"Bless you, Amy! You're here? I thought you wouldn't have come in such weather. I didn't think to look for you inside."

"I wanted to get home so badly," said the young traveler. She put the infant into its father's arms. The baby began to kick and coo with delight. "It didn't seem like it was going to rain when we left London. I wouldn't have come in that case," she added.

"Well, I am glad you were able to get a seat inside the coach," her husband said fondly.

"I wouldn't have," said Amy," if it hadn't been for a young gentleman. She looked around to thank her friend again, just in time to see him turn the corner of New Street.

"There he goes! I am sorry he left so soon," she said. On their way home, the wife gave her husband a full account of the incidents in her travels. She told him of her journey from the Bull's Mouth in London to the Hen and Chicks in Birmingham.

One Sunday morning a few weeks afterward, Arthur Sutherland and his sister were walking to church. They passed a young couple. Arthur recognized the lady as the poor woman with whom he had traveled. It was plain that she remembered him, too. In another minute her husband had turned and was at Arthur's elbow.

"Excuse me, Sir," he said. "I want to thank you for your kindness to my wife, Amy. I'm talking about that terrible night the two of you came down from London."

"Don't speak a word about it," replied the youth. "I am glad I was able to help out a little. It isn't worth mentioning. I hope the storm didn't harm your wife any. She certainly got soaked."

"It didn't hurt her at all, Sir. If she had traveled all the way outside of the coach, it might have been terrible. She had gone to London to see her friends. She hardly had enough money left to pay her fare back. It was money out of your pocket, Sir...." After a little hesitation, the man added, "Would it offend you if I offered to pay you back?"

"Don't say anymore about it, my good fellow. I wouldn't think of it."

"Then, Sir, I must thank you for it. I hope I am able to return the kindness some day." Then the man rejoined his young wife.

"That's young Mr. Sutherland," he said. "His father is a very selfish man, they say. The son has a good character and is known for his kindness. It's a good thing that the old gentleman wasn't on the coach that night instead of the young one. You might have been wet through fifty times before he would have said a word to you, Amy."

"What? Is that a new friend you have picked up now, Arthur?" Arthur's sister asked when the short conference was over. "What was that about the coach? Now I know why you had to borrow from me that day after your journey to London."

"Well, never mind now, Jessie. I'll tell you all about it sometime," said Arthur.

Years went by. Arthur Sutherland was now a grown man. Again he was traveling from London to Birmingham. This time, he was taking a different type of transportation. On a bleak winter afternoon, he entered a second-class railway car at Euston Square. He wrapped a railway-blanket around him and exchanged his fur hat for a cap which he took from his pocket. He leaned back in a comfortable corner. Half closing his eyes, Arthur waited patiently for the starting signal.

Arthur was in that kind of dreamy mood in which he barely noticed things around him. That same day he had landed in England, after a long and stormy voyage across the ocean. He had been away for three years and was quite tired of traveling. He felt as if he would never get through the boring, five-hour train ride to get home. His mind had never been more awake, however.

One by one, images rose up before him as he drew nearer home. They mingled fitfully with the memories of his travels in other parts of the world. He thought about the profits and losses he had incurred on his business journey. Other thoughts and images pushed into his mind. Then they all combined to interest him so that he had no hope of getting any much needed sleep.

A partnership in his father's business was an immediate possibility. A home of his own and a wife were also a part of the picture. What a wonderful wife he was going to have. He had waited so long! Arthur had worked long and hard to overcome one obstacle after another which had postponed or prevented the wedding. He had finally overcome them at last. No wonder Arthur Surtherland was in a dreamy mood, yet unable to sleep.

He was so dreamy before the train started that he hardly noticed two other travelers sharing the compartment with him. By the dim light from the oil lamp, he finally noticed that he was not alone. He saw that the person opposite him was a respectable-looking, middle-aged man. By his side was a stout man in a bear-skin coat. His breath smelt suspiciously of strong alcohol. It was unpleasant to be so close to this person with a raspy, loud voice.

Our friend had traveled too far and long to be very curious. He came to the conclusion that it would be wise to keep to himself. Rather than talking with his fellow travelers, he settled himself more firmly in his corner. Once again he let his imagination drift into things of the future.

The train sped along miles and miles of the iron roadway and passed several stations. Meanwhile, the dreamy traveler gradually became aware of his companions. Apparently a conversation about a topic that interested him was passing between them. He began to listen more closely. He heard them talking about events which were common enough at that time but which sounded strange and new to him.

For example, he heard of grand fortunes made in an incredibly short span of time on the railroad stock market. They talked about the mad excitement which had caused the stock market to soar. People were playing tricks and schemes by buying and selling for a quick profit. This was their downfall. Finally, when the market crashed, it ruined hundreds of lives. In their hurry to get rich, they gave up their established businesses. They caused themselves many sorrows. The recent disclosures spread distrust throughout every business circle.

"I don't like it. I never did like this large scale gambling," said the gentleman in the opposite corner. "They had their fingers bitten hard by putting them into the trap. I scarcely pity them. Their families will have to suffer and that's the worst thing about it.

"Well, Mr. Smith," retorted the man with the loud voice and bear-skin coat who sat by Arthur's side. "There has been a good deal of stupidity at the bottom of it all. If you can cheat people, do it, I say. I never thought I'd hear you talk down upon the railroads, however."

"I don't speak against the railroads," said the gentleman in a quiet tone. "I can only say that I am thankful I had so much to do with making them a reality. I don't have the time nor do I care to gamble with them."

"I say," said the man in the bear-skin coat with a secretive tone. He nudged Arthur's side to attract his attention. The train had stopped at a station where their fellow traveler got off for a minute or two. "I say, do you know that man?"

"Can't say that I do," Arthur replied sleepily.

"Ah!" resumed the man, drawing a long breath. "He's a lucky fellow. Why, you must have heard of Alexander Smith, the successful railway man!"

"No, I haven't," said Arthur. "I have been overseas a long time, and have not been in England a full day yet."

"Oh! That explains it. You will hear about him then. Ten or twelve years ago, he was nothing but a Birmingham mechanic. Some lucky idea he had about the railroads made him successful. Now they say he's worth millions. You should just go and look at his factories."

"Oh," said Arthur Sutherland with small interest. At the same moment Mr. Alexander Smith returned.

"Mr. Smith," said the bear-skinned traveler as he resumed the conversation. "There is some excitement in this gambling, as you call it. There was some fun in it while it lasted at any rate. If some lost, others won. It's about fair."

"How many losers were there for each winner, Sir?" replied Mr. Smith rather sharply. "No, Sir, it isn't fair or even close to it. That's the way it will turn out eventually. Look at the bankruptcy list in every Gazette. Tell me what you think about that, Sir."

"Ah!" responded the other. "Things are not fair there. By the way, another of your head workmen is gone, I see. What's his name? I mean the one from Dansburry street."

"Yes, Sir. I am sorry for it. Fifty thousand dollars lost, they say. He wasted all of it in this mad, wild goose chase after railway stock. Yet he did it so secretly. He had such a reputation for wealth and cleverness. Just a week ago his was one of the finest houses in Birmingham."

Something in the tone of the conversation caught the young traveler's attention. The street mentioned was the one his father's business was on. He was curious to know which of his neighbours they were talking about. Meanwhile the conversation went on.

"Perhaps you had money in it, too, Mr. Smith?"

"No Sir, not a penny," was the answer.

"Oh, I fancied you might," said the man in the bear-skin. "You said you were sorry."

"Well, Sir, it is possible to be sorry for others as well as for yourself. I am sorry, too, for the suspicions that are growing towards other businesses. It seems that now everyone will be suspect. That will cause as much trouble as the gambling has. Besides, I am sorry for Mr. Sutherland and his family. For...."

Arthur was jolted out of his land of dreams. Before Mr. Smith could finish the sentence, Arthur interrupted. "Excuse me, Sir. Did you say Mr. Sutherland...," Arthur stopped short. He could not think of a way to ask the question that trembled on his lips.

"I was speaking about Mr. Sutherland, Sir," replied Mr. Smith mildly.

"Not of...that is...you don't mean there is a...Do you mean there is something wrong with Mr. Sutherland's business?"

"By this time, you can't doubt it. You have heard that his name was in yesterday's Gazette and his place is closed. The common report is that Mr. Sutherland has ruined himself with railway transactions. He risked all his money in it, I'm afraid."

"You don't mean Mr. Everett Sutherland?" said Arthur with increasing excitement. He could not conceal it any longer. "Some other person of the same name, maybe? It couldn't be Mr. Everett Sutherland of Dansbury street!"

The reply he received removed all chance of mistake. The young man became thankful now for the dull light of the railway lamp. He was stunned and bewildered by the sudden, unexpected news of his father's ruin. He sank back into his corner again. His pleasant daydreams all vanished. A confused and tangled web of gloomy suspicions replaced them.

Shortly afterwards, the rough-coated man left the train and Arthur became aware that he was being carefully examined by his remaining companion. Before he could hide himself from this unpleasant search, the other man broke the silence.

"I am not wrong, am I?" said Mr. Smith, "in believing that you are Mr. Arthur Sutherland?"

"Certainly, I am Arthur Sutherland," replied the young man. "You have an advantage, Sir. I have never before had the pleasure of meeting you, Mr. Smith."

"Once before we did, but in rather different circumstances. That does not matter now. I must sincerely apologize for the pain I have carelessly caused you. I wasn't aware that you were my traveling companion when I spoke of...."

"It doesn't matter, Sir," said Arthur. "If what you say is true, I would have found it out tonight. A few hours sooner or later make no difference." He again went silent, and his fellow traveler did not attempt to interrupt his thoughts. When the shrill scream of the engine announced that the journey was coming to an end, Mr. Smith spoke once again.

"May I have one word with you, Mr. Sutherland?" he asked respectfully. "I am afraid you will find matters in a sad state. It is strange that you knew nothing of this before. I have been thinking that perhaps I may be able to help you a little. If so, here is my card. Come to see me."

Arthur mechanically took the offered card and muttered a thank you for the man's kind offer. In a few minutes a car was carrying him and his luggage from the railway station to his father's house.

Arthur's heart was heavy as Jessie welcomed him with tears of both sorrow and gladness. "Tell me," he begged. "Is what I have heard this night, true?"

"Dear Arthur, the awful thing you heard is true. We are ruined."

"Our father, how is he, Jessie?"

She shook her head sadly. The mad excitement of the past few months had taken its toll on the old man. It had weakened his mind and body. It was painful to witness. "You are our only hope now, Arthur. Oh, how glad I am you have come back at last."

Arthur Sutherland slept very little that night. He feared that his father's terrible situation would destroy his future. All his hopes and dreams had only recently begun to shed a bright light on his existence. The partnership with his father would be one of poverty and disgrace. The wedding engagement would end in bitter disappointment.

"I am sorry for you, Arthur," said his fiancée's father when Arthur went to his business the next day. "I must say you have behaved honorably in coming to me first. Your own good sense will tell you that you should drop the engagement altogether. You know I did not give my consent to it very willingly at first, and now..."

It only took that unmistakable "and now" to make Arthur return home upset and forlorn.

Arthur Sutherland's arrival; however, was very well received in the business world. He had a good reputation among his father's creditors. They knew that he had no share in making the errors which brought about the failure of the business. His assistance was valuable in taking care of the many important details of the bankruptcy. With honesty and unselfishness, he gave all his time and effort.

One evening Arthur was slowly returning from the bank to his father's house. His business was not finished, but at least the harassing duties of the day were over. Suddenly, a gentleman he vaguely recognized as the companion of his railway journey stopped him.

"I have been expecting and hoping you would take me at my word, Mr. Sutherland. I thought you would come to see me before now. Since you have not, I was just going to find you. Are you through working for the day? If you are and will allow me, I will walk home with you."

Arthur took the offer.

"Now, what are you doing? How are you getting along? I don't really need to ask you this. Everybody I meet speaks with praise about your unselfish efforts to make the most of this disastrous affair. Now that I think about it, I'm pleased that you have not come to see me before now."

"What does he mean?" thought Arthur, but he spoke little. Soon they reached his home.

"Now, Mr. Sutherland," said Mr. Smith when they were settled in the parlor, "May I ask what you intend to do when these affairs are settled?"

Arthur replied that he had no plans for the future. He supposed; however, that he might perhaps work in a trading business.

"I believe your father's business was a good one, Mr. Sutherland. Why not take it into your own hands?"

We shall not relate any more of the conversation of that evening. Arthur found that somehow he had gained the friendship and kindness of a sympathetic and able friend. After an interview, which lasted until quite late, young Arthur entered the room where his sister was waiting for him. He was in a more hopeful frame of mind than he had been since his return home.

A few weeks passed by. It became known that Arthur Sutherland had bought his father's failed business. He planned to expand this business with the advantages and profits of foreign trade. He did not hide the fact that the kind assistance of Mr. Smith had made it possible for him to take this step. The open-handed, but sometimes unpredictable, generosity of that gentleman was no secret. Nevertheless, there was a mystery which remained for months afterwards.

Before we learn how that was solved, let's satisfy the curiosity of some of our readers. They are the ones who think that a story is never finished until there is a wedding. It is left for them to imagine how Arthur Sutherland again courted and finally won the lady of his choice.

"There was a wedding, then?"

"Yes, a very quiet, modest affair. Not at all one you would approve of if you like romantic events. There was a wedding; however, and that is something. Respectful wedding visits were paid and in due time returned."

As our two gentlemen were again visiting in Mr. Smith's drawing-room, this fragment of conversation passed. "Are you saying that you never saw Mrs. Smith before, Mr. Sutherland?"

"No, I never saw her until she did us the honor of calling the other day. Never, at least, that I can remember."

"Look again, Mr. Sutherland, are you quite sure? This girl?" He laid his hand on his eldest daughter's shoulder. "Have you never seen her before?"

The tone of Mr. Smith's voice puzzled Arthur. He repeated that if he had ever had the pleasure of meeting her, his memory had failed him.

"Perhaps, you will refresh our friend's memory, Amy," said Mr. Smith to his wife.

"Don't you remember," asked the lady in a soft, gentle voice, "a dreadful storm on a July night many years ago? Traveling from London on the coach was a poor young woman. She was lightly dressed and had an infant in her arms. Do you remember that?"

"Yes, yes, certainly I do," said Arthur eagerly, for the memory at once flashed into his mind.

"Do you remember the poor woman's alarm and the meanness of the coach-owner? He would have turned her out of the coach and into the rain?"

"That young woman's husband," continued Mr. Smith, "told you that he would find a way to repay you. You showed kindness without expecting a reward or thanks. That man has never happened to meet with you in his travels since, until recently. Tell him, Amy, what you know about this."

"I am that poor woman," said Amy. "This young girl you see here was the infant I carried with me that stormy night."

So it was that the seed of a little kindness, sown years before, sprung up and rewarded the one who planted it. Ecclesiastes 11:1 says, "Cast thy bread upon the waters: for thou shalt find it after many days."

...a sad, lonely woman sat thoughtfully at her evening meal.

Chapter 4

THE ONE TALENT

In an ancient city of England was a large, dreary, old-fashioned house that was once owned by a rich nobleman. Now the run-down building was divided into separate apartments. The new owner rented these to poor, working people. In an upper room of this same old house, a sad, lonely woman sat thoughtfully at her evening meal. She was thinking out loud, as elderly people often do. This is how her thoughts went.

"Well, I've done today's work, but Saturday will be here soon. Let me see...," she said as she dumped all her money out of an old canvas bag. About ten-pence, a six-pence, and a half-crown rolled out onto the table. This was the extent of her savings.

Her cupboard contained nothing more than a half loaf of bread and an ounce of tea. There was some butter and a piece of leftover fish sitting on a plate. She had a bit of beef broth given to her by the people she had worked for that day. This was her complete supply.

A very small fire burned in the grate. She had a reasonably sized pail of coal left down in the cellar and a few sticks. A kind little girl had given them to her. This was the total extent of her fuel.

The old woman slept in an iron bed which filled one corner of the room. Upon it lay a very thin, hard mattress. An old, patched blanket and a blue bedspread covered it. An old wicker chair and a little round beige table reminded her of better days. A tea tray and a tiny, square mirror without a frame sat on an odd-shaped dresser. On a tattered rug on the floor sat a high-backed, old-fashioned chair, which was a gift from her grandmother. These were the sum total of the scanty possessions she called her own.

She had good reason to sigh, then, as she dumped the money into her lap. She thought over all her troubles. The rent would soon be due. Food was short and hard to buy. Work was hard to find, and she didn't have many friends.

She sipped her weak tea and spread a piece of stale bread with some butter. The old lady murmured, "But it won't do any good to worry. I must remember God's Word says to those who walk and speak uprightly, '...bread shall be given him; his waters shall be sure.' Yet it is hard to claim that promise when I am down to my last penny. I see how far I fall short in my conversation and walk. Then it is difficult to believe the good words that Brant read to me last night. 'Seek first the kingdom of God and His righteousness, and all these things shall be added unto you.' Brant! I wonder why he hasn't come yet? It is such a cheerful evening. Maybe he has strolled into the country for a breath of fresh air after his hard day's work. If I weren't so tired, I would do that myself. Standing all day washing clothes tires me out too much. Say, who's that coming up the stairs? I wonder if that is Brant after all."

No, it was only the scruffy old fellow who worked at the wool merchant's. He always came home dirty, and often drunk. He usually wasn't home as early as he was tonight, however. He wasn't a married man, but he never took any notice of the widow when she met him on the stairs. As she looked outside her apartment, she couldn't resist bidding him "good-night." He only replied with a growl, so she sadly shut the door and decided to forget about any visitors.

"If my vision weren't so poor, I would love to read the greatest book of all tonight," she said. Then she looked at her Bible on the table. "He who has afflicted me with failing sight has better blessings in store for me. Perhaps they are even better than receiving this wish."

Saying this, she began to put away her cup and saucer and the little, black teapot. She decided that the tea leaves had no more flavor left in them, so she set them aside for their last use. She would sweep her room with them tomorrow. The widow sat down by the small, high window to catch the rays of the setting sun. She heard footsteps again; this time she was not disappointed. It was Brant.

Brant was an overworked, underfed youth of eighteen. He was a painter in the town. He looked sickly as most painters did at that time. Their kind of work was very unhealthy. To have a job at all, however, was a privilege during this time of widespread poverty. Brant did not complain.

"I hardly expected you tonight," said Mrs. Warner. She looked gratefully into his face. "I thought this first fine evening since the wet weather began would have tempted you to leave the city."

"Oh no. My pleasure and duty are in the city. I have a whole hour free to read to you and poor old Mrs. Clarke before I must go home."

With that the young man retrieved a small, well-worn Bible out of his pocket. He opened it and began to read the parable of the talents with much sincerity. He did not comment much about it. He said, "The gospel is its own interpreter. The lesson taught by this simple and beautiful story is too obvious to need much explanation."

The widow was less than satisfied. She lifted her hands and let them fall back into her lap hopelessly. She pleaded, "But what, what can I do? Surely, Brant, I don't even have the one talent."

Brant smiled. "You don't think, Mrs. Warner, that the talent simply means money, do you?"

"No, oh no!"

"Do you think it means simply intelligence or education?"

45

"Well, I don't know, but I feel I don't have much of either."

"Not much, eh? Well, then you have the one talent, or maybe the half talent. You still have a responsibility. To one person God may give tremendous riches, while to another a brilliant mind, but very little money. One person may be strong and have good health, while another may have little of anything. It doesn't matter how much we have. God will only ask us how we use what He has given us."

"Maybe so. Still, Brant, you would have a hard time finding my talent. It is not in my purse, I know," the widow said, as she took out the little canvas bag and shook it at him. "It's not in my head, I am sure, and my body is not very strong. Finally, my dear boy, I am a poor, lonely woman. I am of no use to anybody. It often seems strange to me when I see death steal a father from his child. It can steal a mother from her helpless baby or a child from his loving parents. Then it leaves a poor, hopeless, unloved creature like me. They would have to beg mock-mourners to follow me to the grave."

"That's not quite as it should be, is it, Mrs. Warner? You must have a hidden talent somewhere. Every being in God's universe has a part to perform and work to do. I am sorry that I cannot discuss this subject anymore, but my time is up. I'll leave you to pray about it and think it over." He bid her good night as he stood up to leave.

Just as she admitted, Mrs. Warner was a lonely, depressed widow. She was one of those poor people who like to keep to themselves. She had known better days. She did not wish to stop below her level to become friends with anyone who was more needy than she. She existed in her own-world and didn't associate with many people. She was not at all selfish or hard-hearted. She had merely become poor, and poverty had changed her. She did not have much hope for anything. As long as she could earn enough money by washing and ironing to buy bread, she was content.

When she couldn't earn enough to survive on anymore, then she must go to the workhouse. She knew that hour was soon approaching. "That is that," she told herself.

In spite of her thoughts, she had long known the truth. She loved it to a certain degree, but she had loved it more in earlier days. That was before her heart ached so grievously and her path had become so difficult. Nevertheless, she still loved the truth. She did not appear to be a happy Christian. Everyone who saw poor widow Warner thought she was a woman of a pitiful spirit. She was not unhappy because she was not an active Christian. She was unhappy because she didn't fill her important place in life. She felt as a mere beast before the Lord because she had hidden her talent.

The pale, thoughtful visitor who had just left her apartment had little reason to be happier than widow Warner. He had a deaf father, a caring but cross-tempered step-mother, step-brothers and step-sisters, and only one real sister. She meant everything to him. There was a beauty in their love, because they had been through many sorrowful times together. His sister earned her living by sewing at home, where she also helped take care of the younger children.

Brant first met Mrs. Warner while she was washing clothes at a house where she regularly worked. He overheard her complaining that she couldn't read as she used to. Brant walked her home that night. When they arrived at the foot of the staircase to her apartment, he offered his help. He said, "Mrs. Warner, if you would like me to come in and read to you once in awhile, just say so. It would delight me to do it."

She whirled around in surprise. "I have lived here many years," she said. "You are the first friendly person who has spoken to me. You must mean well because you have nothing to gain from offering your time I am sure. I am very poor and I cannot even pay you with a meal. I would be thankful if you would read to me. The Bible is my greatest comfort. I cannot see well enough to read mine because the print is so small."

After a little more discussion, it was agreed that Brant would come over after work the next night. From that time on the widow eagerly awaited his daily visits. It was the happiest and brightest hour of her day.

After her visitor left that evening, Mrs. Warner did not put out her candle and go to bed as she usually did. She felt slightly offended by him. Naturally, she would have felt this way with anyone else, but Brant was a favorite friend of hers. He had always been very kind to her, but of course he was very young. "What could he mean? I have a talent? Indeed! Why, I have no talent. If I did have one, what is the use of it? Who knows or even cares about me? There is the harsh old man who lives across the hall. He has never given me a decent answer when I speak to him. That woman with the bunch of children on the next floor, she hardly even knows my name. Besides, they are all such dirty people. I would not think of being associated with them. What good would it do if I were friendly to them? I could never associate with the dress-maker's girl, with her vanity and indecent dress!"

While talking to herself in this way, she prepared to lie down on her lonely pillow. She did not feel at all happy, because she could not dismiss the question which weighed on her heart. It was almost a nightmare. "What can I do?" Her conscience knew the answer and replied without hesitation, "Do something." She left for work at seven o'clock the next morning with a growing suspicion that her talent must he somewhere. However, it may be a little rusty.

The old lady saw a girl standing in the doorway. She was a dirty, messy, little creature. This was the kind Mrs. Warner liked least. She had stringy hair and clothes that didn't match. There was a blue glass bead necklace tied with dirty tape around her even dirtier neck.

"Please let me by," said the widow somewhat crossly.

The child looked pitifully up to the widow and said pleadingly, "Mother's so sick. She's been sick all night and father's gone for the doctor. I've come to find someone to help."

"You left your mother alone?"

"Yes, but the other children are there."

The widow turned around and knocked at the sick woman's door which stood slightly open.

"May I come in?" she asked.

A woman's voice answered, "Yes, please come in."

Now she saw that her work stood plainly before her, even though she had but an empty purse and very little education.

Earlier the old woman had put the sick woman on her list of those with whom she would not associate. The poor woman rose from her bed. She sat by the fire half-dressed, shivering in the cold. She was hardly strong enough to sit in her chair. The little, unwashed tribe of children huddled together in the corner. Only half of them were dressed. The youngest child, a six-month-old baby, was in his mother's lap crying to be fed. What terrified the little girl was obvious enough. Her mother had collapsed in a fit of coughing earlier. The little ones were frightened and cried easily. Mrs. Warner had heard the coughing many times before. The sufferer's husband finally became so alarmed that he ran for the doctor. This was the setting of the useless widow's first experience at helping others.

"I will not be able to work today," she thought with regret. "I will lose my day's pay. If I don't work today, perhaps I will lose several more days' work as well."

The sick woman must have guessed what was passing through the widow's mind. At that very moment she said in a trembling and worried voice, "Please do not leave me yet. The doctor should be here soon, and I am so frightened."

The widow sent the messy little girl to the house of her employer. She could apologize and explain why the widow could not make it that day. Then the old lady sat by her neighbor's chair. She tried to calm her fears and the baby's cries.

Doing an act of charity and turning one's heart toward the distress of another is sure to create love. There is an old saying, "pity is akin to love." Perhaps true pity and kind Christian compassion is love itself. After Mrs. Warner sat by the miserable patient for a little while, she took hold of her hand and asked if she could pray for her. Suddenly, she felt her heart glow with interest and compassion in a way that was unusual for her.

The desperate state of the room amazed her. The disorder made her forget she was missing a day of work and that she would not have bread for tomorrow. She helped the patient sit up on pillows in her uncomfortable bed. She wrapped the baby up in a shawl and gave it to its sister. The little nurse could give it some fresh air. Soon the husband returned with the doctor. He looked more surprised than pleased when he saw Mrs. Warner.

She had always kept herself so distant from her neighbors. His reaction was not at all unreasonable. This time there was tenderness in her voice and humility in her manner. When she told the man that she was willing to stay, he was instantly grateful. Oh, how happy she felt when he approved. Her heart was so light when she remembered the conversation of the night before. It suddenly struck her that she had found her hidden and long overlooked talent! Those who have never made such a sacrifice have no idea of its effect on others.

The children went outside to play and the widow sat by the sickbed. After the medicine had calmed the mother, Mrs. Warner had time to think. She remembered her rent, her lost day's work, and maybe her lost job. She asked this question, "Can God require all this of me, as poor and needy as I am?"

It was a difficult struggle. The widow said very kindly, "Mrs. Parnell, I have made your room as comfortable as I can. I will stay with you all day if there is no one else. Do you have a mother, or a relative, or friend who would come in and nurse you? I would gladly do it myself but I have a hard living to earn. You must understand that I am somewhat anxious to get to work."

When the sick woman heard this, she raised herself up on her elbow. After a fit of coughing, she choked out, "My mother? She lives in London. I have no one from around here that I can think of just now. Please don't leave me today. I'll ask John if one of his sisters or old Mrs. Grant would come. Dear me! She is so edgy with the children. Oh dear!" she pleaded. "Can't you stay?"

When Mrs. Warner saw the feverish excitement of the patient, she regretted having mentioned the subject. Now Mrs. Warner could only comfort her like a lost child. She promised that she would not leave her until they found someone else to take her place.

It was much harder to keep her promise than the widow had counted on. The children were unruly and hungry. The chimney smoked. The patient coughed and the baby screamed constantly. By the time the husband arrived home from work to eat dinner, Mrs. Warner was losing her patience.

While the husband and children were eating, she went to the door to watch for Brant. As he passed by on his way to lunch, she was thankful to see him and explain her problems. Gray haired woman that she was, she asked young Brant for his advice about the situation.

"I will think about it carefully," he said. "I will come by this evening. Then I will tell you if I can find anyone to help nurse the sick woman. Do you think she would see me?

I'm afraid that she has sadly forgotten the 'most important thing.'"

"I don't know. Indeed, her heart seems set on this world, poor thing. I will ask her. We must find someone to nurse her, Brant. I can't lose my job, as you know."

"'Sufficient unto the day are the cares thereof,' Mrs. Warner. Surely you can't leave her today."

Mrs. Warner thought Brant seemed rather cold toward her fears. When he had gone, she went up into her own quiet, private room. She had to escape the confusion of below so she could consider what to do.

Until now, her actions toward the poor woman had been only out of charity. The time had come for her to be charitable because of principle. So she lifted her heart to God and asked Him to help her along the difficult path of self-denial. She humbly asked that He who clothed the grass and cared for the sparrow would not forget her. She was a poor, needy creature. Having dried her tears, she left her little room comforted and strengthened.

The work was not easy now, but it was easier. She was acting from principle and not merely from impulsive kindness. Leaving tomorrow's cares for tomorrow, she attacked the day's work eagerly.

The children were in the way. With some hesitation, she decided to put them in her own neat room. She told them that they were not to make a mess of her household treasures. She did, however, tell Jenny to feel free to use some soap and water while they were there.

It is beautiful to see how the poor often help one another in times of sickness and difficulty. The patient very justly told her husband that she did not know she had such caring friends as she had discovered that day. Besides Mrs. Warner's kindness, one poor woman who lived across the street brought over her own dinner, even if it was only a little broth. A second woman came to offer to watch at night. This lady was so old and crippled she could hardly walk. A third was the most welcome of all and perhaps the most unselfish. She volunteered to take care of the crying baby so its mother might rest better.

Those of you who have not studied the poorer folk should take notice of their lives. They may be poor in worldly goods, but rich in kindness and generosity. We can profit very much from their example. You may be willing to give your help to a friend in times of sorrow and difficulty. You might offer to sit up and watch someone for a night. You may care for a crying child so a friend can get some rest. How often do we see people showing the unselfishness, the generous kindness, or the love and pity that the poor usually show to even those who are strangers?

Brant came in that evening. The poor woman was beginning to feel a little better. She listened with intense interest as the young man read. He read words of warning, peace, and forgiveness out of the Book about which she knew so little.

Brant's sister had come with him. She said she could not stay that night because she had a sick sister at home. It was her turn to nurse the little girl. She would try to come in the morning, however, so Mrs. Warner might get a little rest. It would be Sunday. She had no work to do and her mother promised to allow her to leave.

Brant looked at Mrs. Warner to see how she was handling the idea of losing a night's rest. There was a quiet smile on her face, one he had hardly seen before.

"You were so right last evening, Brant," she said, understanding the meaning of his glance. "I have been wrong for many years and have forgotten the Saviour's example. I have been living only for myself. I thought I held no important position in life. I have no money or education, so I had no purpose except to go to the grave alone."

Night came, and the children were asleep in the little upper room. The lodgers were all asleep. The patient was

53

asleep too, and so the widow sat and watched. She felt very tired, but she was not worn out from doing good. In fact, at dawn on the Sabbath, it is possible that her heart was more at rest than anyone else's in that old city. She was no longer hiding her talent. "Who can tell," she thought. "Perhaps my one talent, if properly used, will bring forth five more talents."

Keeping her promise, Brant's sister came the next day. Mrs. Warner was able to get some rest. The children's faces were washed and much cleaner than usual. Their father took the youngest of them to his sister's house in a nearby village. Jenny stayed to help as much as she could at home.

The widow entered her ransacked apartment that the little Parnells had occupied. She said, "If it were not Sunday morning, and I weren't so tired, I couldn't sleep in this messy room." Since it was Sunday, she straightened the bed. Saving her lecture on untidiness for Jenny until she had rested, Mrs. Warner lay down to sleep.

"Ah!" she thought to herself as she dropped off to sleep. "I wouldn't doubt if that verse Dr. Watts told is as true for the mind as well as the body. 'Satan finds some mischief still, for idle hands to do.' I have been useless and idle, too. Satan has troubled me with doubts and fears all of my Christian life. Useless Christians will never be happy. I have sat idle in a corner for so long that I have become miserable. I must now find something to do in this world to show my gratitude to Jesus Christ. He paid the huge debt that I owed to God. He died for me on the cross, so I might live forever. I am not my own, but I have been bought with a price."

While thinking on these things, she fell into a much deserved sleep.

I looked up and to my surprise, Uncle Dave's carriage was coming toward me.

Chapter 5

GREAT EXPECTATIONS

When I was fourteen years old, I learned that I was going to receive an inheritance. It would have been much better for me if I had not found out until much later in life. This is my Story:

When I was a boy my father worked as a tenant farmer. I never knew my real mother. At least I don't remember her because she died when I was two years old. I was her only child. My father loved my mother very much, but in time he recovered from his sorrow. He was a young man and his home was in need of a woman's care. After being without a companion for a year, he married for a second time.

My step-mother was very kind to me. This was good for me. She had children of her own but she still treated me as one of them.

Her son, Hank, was three years younger than I. He had two sisters. My new mother loved us all the same. If there was any favoritism shown, it was towards me. I can remember many times when she gave me special privileges. My father was kind to all of us. He was not a rich man and his life always seemed to be full of struggles. He had his health, his strength, and a willingness to work. Problems never appeared to bother him.

My father and step-mother were very Godly. They were true Christians. They knew the true source of happiness. The Bible guided their lives. They believed in it and loved it. Even though we weren't rich, we were a very happy family.

Godliness is Great Gain

We received the best education our father could provide. Upon turning fourteen, I finished school and began to work on the farm. I liked this change. I didn't mind working hard and wanted to be a farmer. However, I could have easily forgotten that I was a step-child if it wasn't for Uncle Dave.

Uncle Dave was the brother of my natural mother. He lived far away and came to visit us once in awhile. We were always glad to see him because he was a good, kind man. His only fault was that he did not always use good judgment. Also, he had a strong prejudice against step-mothers, including mine. When problems arose, Uncle Dave would encourage me to complain to my father about my new mother. He thought I lived in terrible conditions. Eventually, these talks had a bad effect on me. They made me insecure for a while. Then I would realize I had no reason to be unhappy. I would forget I had a step-mother until the next time uncle Dave came to visit.

I can easily remember the day when I began to change my mind. I was spreading manure on a field near the road by our farmyard. It was the first time I had done work like this. My father encouraged me and assured me I could do as well as the strongest man on his farm. It was hot and tiring work but I didn't mind. Taking my shirt off, I was using the pitchfork like a man. Soon I heard the sound of horse's hooves on the road. I looked up and to my surprise, Uncle Dave's carriage was coming toward me. I threw down the pitchfork and ran to meet him.

"Hello, Uncle! How are you?" I exclaimed, almost out of breath. I stepped into the road as the carriage approached.

My uncle drew the horses' reins and looked at me in surprise. "Say, Aaron, is that you?"

"Yes, Uncle, it certainly is," I said happily as I held out my work-stained hand to shake his. He would not touch it.

"I'll shake hands with you, young man, after you have been washed. Why in the world are you doing work like this?"

I blushed bright red to the tips of my ears at his cold response.

"Well, I...like it...I think. Uh, because my father told me to do it," I said, shoving my dirty hands in my pockets.

"Your father should be ashamed of himself," my uncle replied. "He's working you too hard. If your mother were alive, this would not be happening. They won't continue to treat you like this if I have my way!"

Not knowing what to say, I kept quiet.

"This is not the kind of work I want my nephew doing," stormed Uncle Dave angrily. I wondered if being in the hot sun too long had put him in a bad mood. Besides, I enjoyed my farm chores.

"I'm going to put a stop to this!" my uncle roared. "I have a right to do so because I'm the trustee of your grandfather's property. Do you know that your grandfather left a fortune which you will inherit when you reach the age of twenty one?"

My grandfather was upset when my father re-married. I knew that grandfather had died when I was five, but I had never heard anything about an inheritance.

"Just as I thought," he said. "That is too bad. I'm going to see what I can do for you. Well, you'll be going back to the house pretty soon, won't you? When you're cleaned up and dressed properly, we will discuss the matter further."

With that, Uncle Dave whipped his horse. His carriage was soon out of sight, leaving me in a cloud of dust. Doubt and confusion filled my mind.

I picked up my pitchfork again, but I didn't want to work in the fields anymore. If I was heir to a fortune, why hadn't someone told me sooner? I looked at my hands.

Uncle Dave would not touch them because he was afraid he'd get dirty.

They weren't very clean and I felt so ashamed. Hot tears stung my eyes.

"He won't ever catch me like this again," I promised myself.

Just then I heard my step-brother, Hank, down the road, whistling a tune. He was coming home from school neatly dressed. I forgot that only three months ago I was glad to finish school so I could begin working. I forgot that in three years Hank would probably be doing this same job. I was angry and jealous. When he cheerfully ran up to me, I told him to get lost. Poor Hank wondered what was wrong. With shoulders sagging, he slowly turned and walked home.

Throwing down my pitchfork, I started for home too. I quickly washed and changed clothes. Then I joined my family at the dinner table. My step-mother was upset about something. It looked as if she had been crying. My father was silent and so was my uncle. It was not a very cheerful situation. I felt edgy and in a tense mood. Even my little sisters could sense that trouble was brewing.

Uncle Dave did not stay long. He remained friendly as usual. My parents seemed calm. The night before he left, Uncle Dave took me aside.

"It was very foolish of me to speak to you as I did the other day, Aaron. I was wrong. Try to forget it all, my boy. Be diligent in your work. Your father is wise and kind. He wouldn't do anything to hurt you. The smartest thing you can do is to learn what he teaches you. Then someday you will be a good farmer."

This wasn't at all what I thought he was going to say. It was difficult to hide my disappointment.

"You said I had a fortune coming to me, Uncle."

"That you do, Aaron. However, I shouldn't have mentioned it without your father's permission. He thought you should first learn how to work and depend on yourself. I was foolish not to realize what he was teaching you. However, what's done is done."

Uncle Dave then told me that my grandfather had left five thousand dollars to me in his will. The money was in a bank where it could earn interest until I was twenty-one. No one could withdraw the money from the bank. By that time my inheritance would be worth much more.

"This will be a wonderful fortune to you, if you know how to use it," instructed Uncle Dave. "If you don't, it will be a misfortune, Aaron. Be wise and be dependable."

I did not heed his warning, however. My brain was spinning. Someday over five thousand dollars would be mine! From that time on I became lazy and selfish. My father knew what had caused the change in me.

One day he asked me to do something that I thought I was too good to do. I rebelled and with foolish pride, I reminded him of my coming inheritance. My father was terribly sorry to hear me talk this way but he was patient and loving with me.

"I see what has happened, Aaron," he said, struggling to cover his hurt feelings. "It is easy to become proud of your inheritance, but I hope you will grow wiser in time. I'm sorry your uncle told you about your 'expectations.' I was sorry he did. I had planned to tell you when the time was right. These kinds of expectations don't help young men. That's why I didn't want to tell you while you were young. Your uncle had a different opinion, however. I hoped you had enough good sense in you not to grow proud and selfish about it. Nevertheless, I see that is not the case. I'm going to tell you something right now. The money your grandfather left you will do more harm than good. It may do all harm and no good, Aaron, if you continue to think about it the way you have been."

My father sternly warned me about allowing the "love of money," which is the "root of all evil," to creep into my heart and choke my character. He warned me about arrogance and about "trusting in uncertain riches." Solomon said that these riches grow wings and fly away like an eagle toward heaven. I was to trust instead "in the living God, who giveth us richly all things to enjoy." Father pointed out the dangers he saw ahead. He urged me to forget about my expectations, be obedient and work hard.

"There are more important things in life than five thousand or even ten thousand dollars," he said. "Money can never buy true happiness or peace."

I considered what he said for a little while, but I was soon thinking of my money again. I didn't even want to get up in the morning to work on the farm. I didn't want to help harvest the fields or drive the horses. The hired boy was made to saddle my pony for me when I wanted to ride.

Finally growing tired of my laziness, Father said to me, "You'd better find somewhere else to work. You are hurting our business because you slow everyone else down."

Little did I care, though. I now hated farming and I longed to see the rest of the world. When I was sixteen, I left the farm and went to work in a store in town. This business appealed to me since it wasn't as hard as farming. I became an apprentice in the shop and earned a small wage. The thing I hadn't counted on, though, was staying indoors in one place all day. Trying to keep busy hour after hour was hard when I was used to doing as I pleased. Since an apprentice must sign an agreement to work for three years, I couldn't leave my job. I stayed at the shop, ignoring everything my employer tried to teach me. It was my determination never to be a shop-keeper. On the day my bondage was over, I hurried home to the farm.

Meanwhile, my step-brother, Hank, was doing very well. He had become an apprentice to a carpenter and was excelling in that trade. Because father did not have the money to help Hank buy a farm, he helped him find a suitable job. My step-sisters also were growing up. They were helping mother with the housework and farm chores. It seemed I was the only member without a goal. It didn't matter much since I had an inheritance coming.

On the day that I turned twenty-one, my uncle Dave made an appointment with the lawyer. I was to finally receive my inheritance. With interest added on, my fortune totaled nearly six thousand dollars. After I was given the money, my uncle Dave took me aside for a serious talk.

"Aaron," he told me, "I did a foolish thing seven years ago. I have always been sorry. You know what I mean. You have been expecting this fortune for a long time and now you have it. What are your plans?"

Irritated, I replied, "I'm going to buy a farm." I didn't like the way this conversation was heading.

"Aaron, listen to me. If your mother had not died, your father would have the inheritance instead of you. Your father's remarriage offended your grandfather. That is why the money was left to you. Your father has struggled through many hard times. He's been through more than you will ever know, and he is still struggling. He didn't tell me to say this, but it is true. I thought you should know.

"Instead of helping your father, you have cost him a lot of time and money. Hank and your sisters will always have to depend on their own efforts to earn a living. You should do something for all of them. If you do, God will bless your fortune. If you don't...," he stopped short. Our meeting was finished, and Uncle Dave left me to sort things on my own.

"Of course I'm willing to help them!" I fumed. Didn't my uncle believe that? "How could I have ever been a burden to my father?" I put those accusing words out of my mind.

Every day I expected my father to say something about needing money. Of course, I was going to be very generous when he asked. Instead of asking for money, he asked me the same question Uncle Dave had asked. What was I going to do now?

I gave him the same answer. "I'm going to buy a farm."

"Very well, Aaron. I will not stop you, but you should wait a year or two. First you need some experience."

The truth was that I wanted to be my own boss. I was sure I had enough knowledge and experience to manage my own business.

For the next few years, I continued to ignore good advice. I hired workmen who took advantage of me while I wasted my time having fun. When my fortune was spent, no one seemed to know where it had all gone. The sure thing was that I had not helped anyone with it. I left the farm in disgrace. That was the end of my expectations.

Meanwhile, my brother Hank had been faithfully working helping our parents with their financial problems. My sisters were comfortably settled. None of them had inherited a fortune. They had all been hard-working, careful, and wise in managing their money. They had faithfully kept at their work. While I had wasted time daydreaming, they had been working. Even more than that, while I looked to the world to satisfy me, they had come to realize that eternity was more important than this life.

In the end, it was good that my expectations came to an end. It brought me to my senses. Now, "by the grace of God, I am what I am." My faith is increasing. Although I never helped my family, they helped me when my money was gone. They helped me out of the pit I fell into because of my pride. How can I ever repay them for this?

The lesson of my story is simple: When used properly, expectations are good and valuable. When they cause a person to throw away dependability, faithfulness and humility, they are ill-used. They are "good if used as a walking-stick; bad when leaned upon as a crutch." Only those who "set their affections on things above," can be truly happy. True happiness can only be found through true repentance, and forgiveness by faith in the Lord Jesus Christ.

Only they can look forward, "To an inheritance incorruptible, and undefiled, and that fadeth not away, reserved in heaven for you, who are kept by the power of God through faith unto salvation ready to be revealed in the last time," 1 Peter 1:4-5.

Mr. Bentley rang the doorbell and tenderly gave his daughter a last kiss.

Chapter 6

A LICHFIELD TALE

One evening in the spring, just as it was growing dark, a neatly dressed girl of about seventeen stood at the handsome, iron gate of a gentleman's house in the Lichfield neighborhood. There was no doubt about what was happening. The little blue painted box, the suitcase, the brown paper sack, and her tearful face told the tale. She was leaving home to go to work, and the poor working man holding her hand was her father.

"God bless you, Anne! Keep a smile on your face. Don't expect too much from this change and don't get discouraged easily. Every path has hidden dangers, child. Take comfort there is a God who knows where these dangers are. He even cares for the sparrows. Don't forget the words of your mother. We can all find the secret to happiness if we look to Jesus for it. Jesus said in Matthew 6:33, 'But seek ye first the kingdom of God, and his righteousness; and all these things shall he added unto you.' Good-bye, Anne."

Mr. Bentley rang the doorbell and tenderly gave his daughter a last kiss. As the father turned towards home, he brushed the tears from his eyes. This was the first time his oldest daughter had left home and he felt sad. When he arrived home, her mother was anxiously waiting. She wanted to know how Anne had handled the good-byes and if she had lost any courage.

"Well, she can come back home if she wants to. That's one comfort," said the mother as they sat down to their simple meal. "Not all poor servant girls can say that. I wish they could."

Anne was admitted to the house of her new employer. After being shown her quarters, she was put to work. The cook and housemaid eyed her suspiciously as if she were an intruder. They examined her curiously, trying to remember her among the many girls interviewed for the job. Anne informed them that she had never been to the house until now. With that they realized that they had never seen her before. Mrs. Fenn, due to some household policy of her own, had hired Anne in her father's home. For now, she was to be the housemaid's assistant. When she gained experience, she would be the young ladies' parlor maid.

Most people have had a particular goal at some point in their lives. Anne lived in a busy and poor, though respectable home. She had always thought that her wish would come true if she could become a well-paid servant in a gentleman's household. She was not the only one who had confused worldly riches with happiness and peace. In Anne's eyes, to be rich was to be happy. We shall see how soon she learned that she was wrong.

Anne's greatest desire was to wait on tables. However, Ellen the housemaid was certain that she would be awkward. She kept Anne busy with a needle and many different jobs involving the young ladies. At last, Sunday night came and the housemaid was gone. In her absence it was Anne's responsibility to set the table. She set it and was very pleased with the job she had done.

Supper was the most important meal to Mr. Fenn. He lived a distance from his place of business. His fashionable sons and daughters begged him to eat lunch with the family everyday. Mr. Fenn did not want to do this, so he ate lunch in town. He would return home at seven and have a cup of coffee. Then at ten he would have his old-fashioned, late supper.

He was a man of simple tastes and education. There are now people in town who nod importantly to him when he passes on his fine horse on his way to work. One or two older ladies remember when Jack Fenn was little. He was a messenger for Barker's office in Greenwood. They told of how he would peep through their muslin curtains and gaze longingly at the glimpse of blazing fire and hot rolls. More than once, they tapped on the window and invited him in. They led the pale-faced, fatherless lad into the hall and warmed him. They gave him a cup of tea, a slice of bread with butter, and kind words. He eventually became a partner in that same business. Now he passes by the house as a rich man instead of a poor, hungry boy.

He had arrived at Barker's office filled with dreams as a young boy. Like Anne, Mr. Fenn had mistakenly thought that the ideas of happiness and wealth were the same. Life was easier when he had only a dry crust on which to chew. Now he was a rich lawyer with money in the bank and a greedy family at home.

"My master looks very serious," thought Anne as she waited on the family that night. "The mistress does, too. Somehow it doesn't seem as joyful as our Sunday lunches do. I will go home next Sunday." She had begun to long for home already, though she knew very little food was served at the meals. Butter was a rare treat. Most times they ate their homemade bread plain.

There was one member of Mr. Fenn's family who Anne hadn't seen until that night. Since she had heard nothing but good things about him, she wondered why they called him, "Poor Mr. Edward." He looked like the only really happy one in that little group.

Sometimes the girls were cheerful, but tonight they were cross, and one of them had been crying. They were upset because their normally indulgent father was hesitating about whether to let them stay a month in town at an expensive hotel. The oldest son was not there, and the third child was only a young boy. He was grumpy because everyone else was.

Edward was the only one who looked happy and content. What did he have that made him so much happier than the rest? He had a thin, weak body and his small figure was bent and deformed. A fever had attacked him years ago and had made him almost completely deaf. He would never again enjoy conversing with his family or special friends.

Sadder yet, he would never again be able to hear the beautiful, sweet sound of music. He was trained to be a musician, and he was an excellent performer and composer. Music had now become to him what the sun is to the blind. It was a gift he knew existed, but he could never share and enjoy it with others.

At first, the loss of his hearing was terribly hard to bear. As time went by, he heard a sweet whisper of love and mercy in his aching heart. This reminded the young man of Hebrews 12:5, "My son, despise not thou the chastening of the Lord, nor faint when thou art rebuked of Him: For whom the Lord loveth he chasteneth, and scourgeth every son whom he receiveth." This was the secret of his joy; a lesson he had learned in the school of sorrow. The teaching of the Holy Spirit convinced him of sin, which taught him that, "...by grace are ye saved through faith," Ephesians 2:8.

Anne was thinking quite hard as she looked at poor Edward's face. A sharp hint not to listen to conversation but to attend to her duties brought her to attention. Soon the task of waiting at the table became easy. Anne was a quick, efficient girl. Mrs. Fenn said she would soon be a very good servant.

First impressions are often wrong. It is not necessary to relate what Anne told her parents when she went home that first Sunday. Instead, let's peep into her family's parlor after she had been working for nearly six months. We will pick up the conversation there.

"Oh yes, I suppose I'm happy, but I wish I lived with people who were a little more content and cheerful. Look at my mistress for example. It's not that she criticizes me, but she always looks so sad," said Anne.

"Well Anne, perhaps she has a good reason," said her mother. "'The heart knows why it is bitter,' my girl."

"Reason!" Anne laughed. "Mother, if you saw her beautiful house and all her dresses, rings, and jewelry, you wouldn't think so. She has a pony and carriage all her own. She has nothing to do all day except please herself. Oh! If I were her, would I be happy? Of course, I would!"

"Are you really happy now, Anne?" asked her father with sarcasm in his voice.

"Why should I be very happy? There are so many people I must please."

"Well, that is your problem. Who knows, maybe your mistress has as many people to please as you do. This much I know. There's not an earthly blessing God gives us to which He does not attach a weight. This prevents us from forgetting Him and becoming completely satisfied with worldly joys. Children are wonderful joys, but they require tremendous care. Sometimes they cause much sorrow. Riches are excellent blessings, no doubt, but with riches come many wants that never before existed. 'Rich enough' is a rare state to find. Anne, you look as if you still don't believe me. I am telling you the experiences thousands of rich men have had. There are better things for which to pray than money and food. Well, you'd better go. It's after eight, and you are supposed to be back by nine."

Anne left home with even more mixed feelings than when she first went to work. She began to wonder if the meal of dry bread and tea she had just left, with love and peace, was happier than those in her master's house. Proverbs 15:17 says, "Better is a dinner of herbs where love is, than a stalled ox and hatred therewith."

It wasn't even the end of the year, but the Fenn's were making large preparations for an especially elegant occasion. Mrs. Fenn's daughters complained that their friends were saying they were odd for not having big dinners. So, the Fenns purchased new china dinner plates and prepared to host a lovely feast. Mrs. Fenn solemnly declared she had no desire to go to such trouble. However, she believed the girls should be more accepted by other people, and so she persuaded their father to agree.

Mr. Fenn thought it was a bad idea from the beginning. It would surely lead to other expensive parties. In spite of his misgivings, the ladies planned a magnificent dinner party. Anne was glad to have her share in the excitement. She was usually happy, but she also had her moments of sadness. She couldn't see the beautiful, new, lace dresses or the new bracelets that Mr. Fenn gave each of the girls, without wishing she could wear such expensive items.

Anne suddenly had a depressing thought. She would never be like Mrs. Fenn's daughters. She would always be a poor servant girl. She would never be able to wear expensive clothing. She would always be required to wear a white apron and a little cap instead of a fine, large hat.

Anne was standing in the kitchen serving breakfast on the morning of the dinner party when the postman and her oldest brother, Tom, arrived. Before she could speak to Tom, she had to take the letters upstairs. Then the housemaid asked her to clear the breakfast table. This gave Anne time to notice that the readers found some of the letters to hear unpleasant news.

"How disappointing! Mr. Janson has written to say he can't attend," said Mrs. Fenn. Mr. Janson was a world traveler. He was to be the most important guest at the party. This was only the first disappointment. Anne learned then that dinner parties are not without their troubles.

There was a worried look on Mrs. Fenn's face as she read over another letter.

Edward was curious to know if the letter was from Frank. He put his arm kindly around his mother's waist.

Feeling the beating of her heart, he looked tenderly into her face and saw that she was troubled.

Anne was an intelligent, observant girl. She plainly saw that a rich mother could have greater sorrows than being short of money for the week, or having little food. She felt sorry for her mistress.

She returned to the hallway and realized her brother was still waiting. "Well, Tom, what brings you here today?" asked Anne. "I'm very busy. I can hardly spare a minute."

Her brother said, "Mother sent me to tell you that all the children except me and Hannah are sick. She isn't sure, but she thinks it's the measles. Also," he lowered his voice, "Mother would be grateful if you could send her some money. Father doesn't have much work. On Saturday he only brought home thirty dollars, instead of fifty. Mother needs medicine for the sick ones. Please, Anne, can you send some money?"

"Tom, I would, but I have only four dollars in my purse.

"Why, I thought you would have made a lot of money working here," said Tom pestily.

"Well, so what if I have?"

"You eat here for nothing," said Tom, eyeing the servants' breakfast table heaped with food.

"I do buy my own clothes, Tom. I spent too much money on them this summer that is true. I will ask my mistress to let me have some of my wages in advance since it is almost payday. I'm sure she won't mind."

She quickly ran upstairs, but her request for money came at a bad time. The letter from Frank told of his heavy debts and great difficulties. Mrs. Fenn was crying. Mr. Fenn stood holding the open letter in his hand. His face showed his disappointment. Frank was his oldest son. He was Mr. Fenn's hope and pride. The letter revealed Frank's ungratefulness, extravagance, and selfishness.

When she entered, Anne was silent and nervous. After a short time she said, "Ma'am, may I have part of my wages today?"

"Your wages! They are not due."

"I know ma'am, but I have bad news from home. All of the children are sick with measles."

"You must not interrupt me. I can't help you right now. I have enough problems of my own. Besides, I make it a rule never to pay servants' wages in advance. Leave the room."

Tears of frustration stung her cheeks as she hurried downstairs. Putting all the money she had into her brother's hand, she shoved him out the door. She promised to run home at night if she could get away.

"Yes, please come Tom begged. "Little Charlotte is very sick with her cough. Mother is worried. Come if you can." The poor boy walked home sadly, wondering how money could be so hard to get in that house of plenty. He had seen bright jelly and oranges and lemons in jars on the pantry shelf. He thought how nice it would be to take some home for the feverish, moaning children.

It was a worrisome, anxious day for the rich; and a hard, trying one for the poor. The rich mother, with the wayward prodigal son, had to put her sorrow behind her. She had to prepare for a festive dinner while her aching heart held only bitterness. The poor woman, with her sick children and her fearful thoughts, went from pillow to pillow. She tried hushing and comforting her children. She was often ready to drop from weariness and hearing their cries during this time of hardship and trial. At just such a time she heard the voice of the Spirit she knew so well saying, "...be content with such things as ye have: for He hath said, I will never leave thee, nor forsake thee," Hebrews 13:5.

The day went on. Anne's tears fell on the young lady's dress which she was mending. Mrs. Fenn, who was looking for her, entered.

"Why are you crying?"

"I am crying, ma'am, about mother and the children. Please, Ma'am, could I quickly run home after the guests are all here?"

"That's impossible! Measles are very serious. All my children have had them. It is a good thing they are getting it over with. Please don't worry yourself about such a silly thing." She sent Anne off to give a message to a lady who lived about a half-mile away.

This errand seemed unimportant to Anne. The message was that Miss Fenn hoped Miss Glover would bring a particular music duet. Miss Fenn was afraid she would forget. Anne had to wait in the Glover's kitchen, because Miss Glover was busy and could not be interrupted. This gave Anne time to think.

"If riches will make me cold and hard-hearted, I hope I'm never rich and selfish. How could mistress, being a mother too, speak so coldly about my poor mother's trouble? It's not easy to care for sick children without help."

Anne thought a little more. Then her conscience spoke to her. "I shouldn't be too hard on my mistress. Was I kind and considerate? Did I practice self-denial by spending all my wages on myself? I spent it all just to satisfy my own wants."

Anne did not know herself very well. If she did, she would have been more considerate of her fellow-man.

Five o'clock came. The lace dresses were put on. Because she was so homesick, Anne did not envy them. Anne watched her sorrowful mistress sweep down the staircase in her splendid satin dress. Anne tried to pity the heart that ached beneath the dress, but it was difficult for her. Carriages came and went. Compliments and introductions were exchanged. When all the guests were seated, the master of the house had not yet arrived.

As the clock struck six, a carriage drove up. It was Mr. Fenn. It relieved everyone to hear his voice. The cook had known the master for years. When she heard his voice in the hall, she shook her head and said, "All is not right."

All was not right. He said that he felt very ill, but he would dress and come down to dinner. He begged his wife not to worry about him.

As everyone sat down to a delicious meal at the Fenn's residence, Anne's poor father was entering his own cottage door. A scene of suffering lay before him. Dear little Charlotte was the weakest of the seven children. She had caught pneumonia. She was very sick and could hardly breathe.

"Nothing but a miracle could save her," said the doctor as Mr. Benny entered the room. The wife, exhausted from her day's worries, was sitting by the fire. She was vainly trying to rock her youngest baby to sleep.

Anne was right. There was a contrast between the sickness in the nursery of the rich lady and that of the cottage mother. The contrast was not all in favor of the rich lady.

Father and mother now sat down to watch and comfort one another. Tom had gone to get a few oranges. His sister, Hannah, had become ill as well. She was lying down to rest.

Suddenly, they heard a knock at the door. It was Mr. Edward Fenn. The news of the Bentley's troubles had touched his heart. He would rather comfort a suffering stranger than feast with friends. He had left the dinner table after the ladies had gone into the parlor. This surprised no one, since he was unable to join in the conversation. He was soon at the side of the sufferers.

Edward's face glowed with love and sympathy. With a tender voice, he told them about God's gracious love which he himself knew. He comforted them, and he reminded them that God would supply all their needs. When he came through the door, it was as if an angel was ministering to them. He pointed out Scriptures to the hurting ones which told them of God's faithful promises.

He returned home with a light heart. He had done what he could do. He had given them money for their needs. Because his life was very simple, he had few needs of his own. He firmly believed that having money was not the way to achieve happiness. As he approached his home, he thought of the fearful, aching hearts there. He felt a wave of compassion for the rich father of a thankless son.

The dinner party was soon over, and the pretending ended. The selfish, worldly guests thought it was nothing to eat so much food. They criticized the Fenn's and their lavish party among themselves. Everyone was tired, bored, and restless. When all the guests had gone, the master of the household sat until long after midnight in the brilliantly lighted room. His defeated appearance worried Mrs. Fenn. She urged him to come to bed, but he wanted to be alone. He told her that he would be upstairs soon.

Edward could not rest. He would sneak to the door on tiptoe to see if his father had moved. Edward thought he was asleep. Mr. Fenn sat still with his head resting on the back of the chair. After a long time, Edward could not contain the fear he felt.

"Father!" he cried again and again.

There was no reply.

One glance at his father's face told him the truth. The long-dreaded stroke had come at last. The morning's upsetting news had brought it on. After that night, Mr. Fenn lived as a broken-hearted, helpless invalid.

Anne Bentley went to her father's house the following day. Her small sister was better and had begged to see her. Anne said, "Oh, Mother! I see what sorrow sin has brought into this world. Neither riches nor poverty can ward them off. I used to wonder what you meant when you said 'the secret of happiness is in serving the Lord.' Now I'm seeing the truth. Jesus said of all our earthly necessities, 'But seek ye first the kingdom of God, and His righteousness; and all these things shall be added unto you. Take therefore no thought for the morrow: for the morrow shall take thought for the things of itself. Sufficient unto the day is the evil thereof,'" Matthew 6:33-34.